The Dog
Who Wanted
to Play

by Fred Ash

Illustrated by
Kristina Shvedai

Siretona
Creative

Dedicated to Cohen
and other children who love animals

THE DOG WHO WANTED TO PLAY © 2020 by Fred Ash.

Published by Siretona Creative
November 2021

https://www.siretona.com/thedog-fredash

Ash, Fred, author.
         The Dog Who Wanted to Play / written by Fred Ash; illustrated by Kristina Svedai

ISBN 978-1-988983-37-0 (Hardcover)
ISBN 978-1-988983-36-3 (Audio)
ISBN 978-1-988983-35-6 (eBook)
ISBN 978-1-988983-34-9 (Softcover / Paperback)

Book design by Fred Ash and Colleen McCubbin
Cover design by Kristina Svedai

Printed in Canada

Distributed to the trade by The Ingram Book Company

Tommy was
afraid of Dog.

Dog had big teeth and sharp claws.
His bark was like thunder.

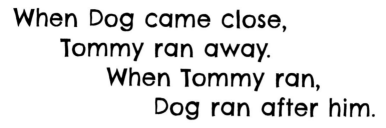

When Dog came close,
Tommy ran away.
When Tommy ran,
Dog ran after him.

He ran down
the streets.

He ran by the bus stop.

He ran into the grocery store.

He ran through the school.

He ran along the path
beside the river.

He ran from Dog
because he was afraid.

Tommy hid from Dog
in the street.

He heard the people say,
"What a beautiful dog."

He hid from Dog
in the park.

He heard the workers say,
"What a magnificent Dog."

Tommy hid from Dog in the playground. He heard the children say, "What a nice dog."

He saw them touch Dog's fur.

But Tommy was afraid
and ran away.

Behind him he thought he heard
Dog's paws hitting the pavement.

He thought he felt Dog's breath
breathing on his neck.

He even thought he heard
Dog's voice say, "Tommy,
don't run away; stop and play."

But Tommy was afraid and ran on.

He crossed a bridge,
and Dog was no longer in sight.

He sat beside a stream and suddenly felt all alone.

He ran to his friends,
but they were tired of playing.

He went to the ice-cream shop but it was no fun eating by himself.

Then he heard the sound of paws on pavement. He saw the shadow of Dog, and he began running again.

He ran fast. Dog ran faster.
Dog seemed to be everywhere.

Tommy thought
he heard the voice again:
"Don't run away; stop and play."

It grew dark.
Street lights came on.
Shadows fell across the road.
Tommy could not run anymore.
He was out of breath.

He looked around.
He did not recognize the street.
He did not recognize the houses.
He did not recognize the playground.

Tommy was lost.

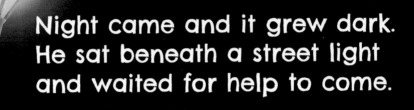

Night came and it grew dark.
He sat beneath a street light
and waited for help to come.

He waited
          and waited
                    and waited.

In the darkness Tommy heard
the sound of footsteps.
No, it was not footsteps.
It was PAW steps!

He looked into the shadows
and saw something VERY BIG.

It was Dog.

Tommy's heart beat faster.

Dog came closer.
He stopped beside Tommy
and looked straight
into Tommy's eyes.

Then Dog sat beside him.

They sat together
for a long, long time.

Two mean-looking men came by.
Dog barked like THUNDER
and showed his big teeth.
The men ran away.

A hungry coyote crept out of
an alley. Dog growled and
showed his big claws.
The coyote slunk
back into the
darkness.

Tommy began to feel a lot safer.
Dog's bark and fiery eyes
comforted him.

He reached out his hand
and gently touched Dog's fur.
It was soft and warm.

The night grew colder. Dog and
Tommy moved closer to each other.
Tommy put his arm around Dog
and allowed the warmth
to soak into his body.

"Why was I so afraid of
you?" Tommy asked.
Dog barked, but
not like thunder.
Tommy thought it
sounded like
laughter.

A police car stopped in front of them. A woman stepped out. "My name is Officer Angela," she said in a friendly voice. "Are you Tommy Francis?"

"Yes, Ma'am," said Tommy.

"And is this your shepherd?" she asked, looking at Dog.

"No, he is just Dog. He doesn't belong to me," said Tommy.

Then Dog turned to Tommy and gave him a big, wet, doggy kiss-lick.

"Well, he may not be yours, but I think you are his," said Officer Angela. "Come, I will take you home."

Officer Angela opened the door of her police car and let Tommy in. Dog jumped in beside him.

As they drove homeward Tommy was sure he heard a voice say, "Tomorrow we can play."

THE END

From the Author

The Dog Who Wanted to Play was inspired by the 19th century poem "The Hound of Heaven" by Francis Thompson.

Like Aslan in C.S. Lewis' *Chronicles of Narnia*, Dog, the good shepherd, cares even for those who run away from him.

Author

Fred Ash is a former elementary school teacher with a BEd and a BA (Hon.) from Memorial University, NL. He is a former editor of children's and teen magazines, with a Certificate in Magazine Journalism from Ryerson University, Toronto. Fred has a master's degree in curriculum design from Tyndale University, Toronto. In retirement he lives in Calgary, Alberta, with his wife, Shirley, where they both volunteer at their church.

Illustrator

Kristina Shvedai is a digital artist and graphic designer, and the creator of many illustrations for children's books. She studied graphic design at the computer academy "Shag" and digital illustration at ArtCraft School. She lives with her husband and two children near Kyiv, Ukraine. Follow her on Instagram @art_vedi.

Find out more! www.fredash.ca